JR. CHAPTER BOOK

THE
BAILEY SCHOOL
KIDS

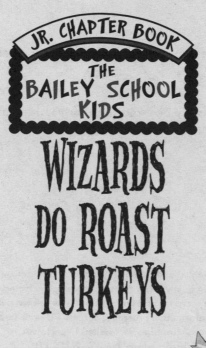

JR. CHAPTER BOOK

THE
BAILEY SCHOOL
KIDS

WIZARDS DO ROAST TURKEYS

by Marcia Thornton Jones and Debbie Dadey
Illustrated by Joëlle Dreidemy

SCHOLASTIC INC.
New York   Toronto   London   Auckland   Sydney
Mexico City   New Delhi   Hong Kong   Buenos Aires

To my mother, Thelma K. Thornton,
who taught me the true meaning of Thanksgiving!
—M.T.J.

To Zachary and Alex Dohr, two special boys
—D.D.

To my beloved fairy Grand-Maman
—J.D.

ISBN - 13: 978-0-545-00235-6
ISBN - 10: 0-545-00235-4

12 11 10 9 8 7 6 5 4 3 2 1   7 8 9 10 11 12/0

Printed in the U.S.A.
First printing, November 2007

CONTENTS

CHAPTER 1: NICE   7

CHAPTER 2: LIZA'S HOUSE   11

CHAPTER 3: NANA-NANA-BOO-BOO   17

CHAPTER 4: TURKEY CHEF   22

CHAPTER 5: POOF!   27

CHAPTER 6: CRYSTAL BALL   32

CHAPTER 7: A FAKE   37

CHAPTER 8: GOBBLE, GOBBLE   43

CHAPTER 9: TURKEY HUNT   46

CHAPTER 10: TROUBLE WITH A CAPITAL T   52

CHAPTER 11: TRUE   57

1

NICE

"This is going to be fun, fun, FUN!" Melody said. She skipped down the sidewalk. A cold November wind blew leaves across her path.

She had to wait for her friends Howie and Eddie to catch up. Both boys walked as slow as snails.

"This is going to be boring," Eddie moaned.

Howie nodded and groaned.

Melody shook her finger at Howie and Eddie. "It's very nice of Liza's family to invite us over for Thanksgiving."

"Thanksgiving is boring," Eddie said.

"At least there will be good food," Howie added. "I like pumpkin pie."

"Halloween was much more fun. Candy tastes a hundred times better than pumpkin pie," Eddie said.

"Plus," Eddie added.
"You get to dress up in scary
costumes and say, BOO!" Eddie
jumped in front of Melody. She
didn't even bat an eyelash.

"You don't scare me,
Eddie," she said. "Besides,
Thanksgiving is more about
friends and family than food."

9

Eddie groaned. "That means I'll have to be polite."

"It won't hurt you to be nice," Melody said.

Eddie fell on the ground. "I'm sick from niceness. Save me!"

SAVE ME!

2

LIZA'S HOUSE

"I knew Liza had a big family," Howie said when the three friends made it to Liza's. "But not THIS big."

Kids ran around the front yard throwing a football. Grown-ups filled the porch.

The front door stood open with people going in and out.

"This might not be so bad after all," Eddie said with a grin.

"Hi!" Liza waved to her friends. "Happy Thanksgiving. You'll never believe who's here."

"Our teacher, Mr. Zep?" Melody guessed.

"The President?" asked Howie.

"Santa Claus?" Eddie said.

Liza laughed. "No, silly.
It's my great-aunt Zelda's new
husband, Great-uncle George.
He's a magician."

"Can he pull rabbits out of
hats?" Howie asked.

"And make handkerchiefs
come out of his sleeve?" Melody
asked.

"Who cares about that?"
Eddie asked. "Can he make
teachers disappear?"

Liza shrugged her shoulders.
"I'm not sure what he can do,
but Great-aunt Zelda says he's
very talented."

"It must be cool to be a magician," Melody said. "When can we meet him?"

"He's putting on a magic show for everyone in a little while," Liza told them. "But right now he's cooking the turkey."

"Magicians roast turkeys?" Howie asked.

Liza nodded. "In my family they do."

"Who cares about turkey?" Eddie said. "Let's PLAY BALL!"

Without even saying hello to Liza's family, Eddie ran to join the touch football game.

"Eddie can be so rude," Melody said with a sigh.

"One of these days," Howie said, "somebody should teach him a lesson."

They were so busy watching Eddie, they didn't notice that someone heard every word they said.

3

NANA-NANA-BOO-BOO!

Eddie didn't like rules.
He didn't like playing fair. He
just wanted to have fun. Liza,
Melody, and Howie watched him
play from the porch.

Eddie ran in front of Liza's
aunts. He zoomed by Liza's
cousins. Eddie grabbed the
football from Liza's grandfather
and ran across the goal line.

"Touchdown!" Eddie yelled.
He did a little victory dance.
"Who's the best?" he chanted.
"I'm the best! Nana-nana-nana!"

I'm the best!

"Eddie!" Melody said from
the porch. "Be polite."
Howie nodded. "Remember
your manners."

If Eddie had any manners, he forgot them. He pushed. He shoved. He stole the ball. He raced into the end zone. Each time he did a happy dance and sang at the top of his lungs, "I'm the best! I'm the best! I'm the best, best, BEST!!! Nana-nana-boo-boo!"

Before long, no one wanted
to play with Eddie.

"We're going to watch
television," the cousins said.

"We're going to help
decorate the house," the
aunts said.

"We're going to dust and vacuum and take out the trash," the uncles said.

Later, Eddie

Eddie was all alone holding the football. He threw it to the ground. "Fine with me," he grumbled. "I'm hungry. Where's the food?"

"There are snacks inside," Liza said. "I'll show you."

4

TURKEY CHEF

Eddie didn't wait for Liza. He raced up the porch steps. He zipped through the door. He ran down the hall into a big dining room.

"Look who just appeared," said a tall man with a long gray beard. He held a platter piled high with turkey. He wore a tall white hat and a long chef's apron.

His apron had pockets all over it.

One of the top pockets was smoking.

Another one sounded like it was popping corn.

Eddie thought one of the side pockets was wiggling.

"I'm hungry," Eddie told the chef. "Do you have anything other than turkey?"

"Well," said the chef as he placed the platter on the table. "Let's see." He reached into a pocket and pulled out a doggy bone.

"What do you think I am?"
Eddie asked. "A puppy?"

"No, no," said the chef.
"Of course not." He patted
another pocket. "Perhaps this
will do." He pulled out a bundle
of green beans and held it out
to Eddie.

"Green vegetables!" Eddie
gasped. "Yuck! Don't you have
any candy?"

"I see," said the chef. "Then how about this?" He tapped a wooden spoon on the table three times.

POP!

ZING!

POOF!

A huge flash filled the room.

Eddie wasn't sure, but he thought he saw a pile of cookies and a big bowl of candy on the table. He shook his head just as his friends walked into the room.

"Did…did…did you see that?" he asked his friends.

"See what?" Liza asked.

But when Eddie looked back at the table, all the treats were gone.

And so was the chef.

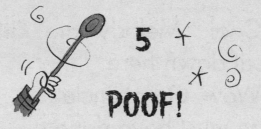

5

POOF!

Liza tugged on Eddie's coat. "Take off your coat," she said. "Great-uncle George is going to do his magic act now." Melody and Howie followed Liza and Eddie downstairs to the basement.

"Cool," Melody said. "It's magical down here."

"Wow, Great-uncle George must have done all this," Liza said. "It doesn't even look like our basement anymore."

"I wish my bedroom looked like this," Howie said.

Twinkling stars hung from the ceiling. A round moon shone above their heads. Fog covered the floor so that the kids couldn't even see their feet.

Liza's relatives were crowded into the basement, waiting for the show to begin. "Where's Great-uncle George?" Liza asked.

Eddie didn't care about Great-uncle George. His eyes were glued to the table full of chips and dips. "Snacks!" he yelled. "That's what I've been looking for."

POOF! A puff of smoke filled the room before Eddie could grab a snack.

POOF!

When the smoke had cleared, a man stood at the foot of the steps. Eddie knew exactly who it was— the turkey chef.

He was still wearing his baggy apron, but he wasn't carrying any food. Instead, his right hand held a shiny glass ball. He plunked the glass ball down on an empty table.

"I can't wait to see the show," Liza whispered to her friends. Liza's great uncle threw glittering dust across the room. It floated over everyone's head.

"I shall begin by telling fortunes," Great-uncle George said. "And I'll start with YOU!"

He pointed right at Eddie.

6

CRYSTAL BALL

"Me?" asked Eddie. "I'm not sure I want to have that magician tell my fortune."

"He doesn't look like a magician," Howie said softly as he nudged Eddie toward Great-uncle George. "He looks like a wizard."

"No way! Wizards wear big hats and robes with pockets full of potions. And they carry magic wands," Eddie said.

"Well, he is wearing a hat," Howie said.

"He does have an apron with big pockets," Melody pointed out.

"And he waves that wooden spoon like a wand," Liza added.

Eddie crossed his arms over his chest and said, "I don't believe he's a magician or a wizard. He's nothing but a turkey chef."

Great-uncle George smiled. "Perhaps I can cook up something special for you," he said. "Sit at the table and look into my crystal ball."

Eddie rolled his eyes when the chef waved a wooden spoon over the glass ball. Eddie plopped into a chair and folded his arms over his chest.

The glass ball turned the color of milk as Great-uncle George said, "Flibber-flabber, mishee-mashee, pizzle-pozzle-pop. Your future is clear. Like a knight of long ago, you will come to the aid of a lady in need."

FLiBBER FLABBER
MiSHEE - MASHEE
PiZZLE - POZZLE - POP

"Me? Help a girl?" Eddie sputtered. "NEVER!" He jumped up so fast he knocked into the table.

The glass ball wobbled.

It toppled.

Then it rolled slowly toward the edge of the table.

7

A FAKE

Great-uncle George dove
for the ball. He caught it just
before it hit the floor. He saved
the ball, but he landed right
on top of the table.

Splat! The table, the
ball, and Great-uncle
George fell flat on
the floor.

"Oh, Eddie!" Liza said as she helped her great-uncle off the floor.

"I didn't do anything," Eddie argued.

"Yes, you did," Melody said.

"None of this would've happened if you had remembered your manners," Howie pointed out.

"No harm done. My crystal ball is still working fine," Great-uncle George said.

Eddie couldn't believe his friends were blaming him. He pushed his way to the snack table as Great-uncle George began to tell Howie's fortune.

"You will be a football star," Great-uncle George told Howie. Eddie groaned. Howie might be the smartest kid in the second grade, but he could never beat Eddie at football.

Eddie was eating his third helping of chips and dip when Great-uncle George told Liza's fortune. "Because of you, trouble will come to you and your friends."

Eddie rolled his eyes. Liza never did anything wrong. She didn't even know how to spell the word *trouble*.

Melody was having her fortune told when Eddie filled his plate for the fourth time. "I see a soccer game, but you are not there," Great-uncle George told Melody. Eddie laughed out loud. Everyone knew that Melody wouldn't miss a game for anything.

"Your great-uncle is a fake," Eddie said as the kids got ready to play pin-the-feather-on-the-turkey.

Suddenly, someone screamed from upstairs, "It's ruined. Thanksgiving is ruined!"

8

GOBBLE, GOBBLE

Everyone rushed upstairs to the dining room.

"The turkey is gone!" Liza's mom cried.

"What's Thanksgiving without turkey?" Liza's grandmother asked.

Great-uncle George pulled his long wooden spoon from an apron pocket. "I can whip up peas and beets and Brussels sprouts."

Eddie grabbed Great-uncle George's hand, stopping the wave of his wooden spoon in mid-air. "We can't make a Thanksgiving meal out of v...v...VEGETABLES!" Eddie stammered.

Great-uncle George shrugged. "What else can we do?"

"I'll tell you what we can do," Eddie said. "We must find that turkey!"

FLAP FLAP

9

TURKEY HUNT

Great-uncle George smiled. "What a good idea! Let's all go on a turkey hunt."

"But someone should stay here and clean up this mess," Eddie said.

"Oh, thank you," Liza's mother said. "Eddie, you're my hero!"

My hero!

Eddie opened his mouth to complain, but Melody patted him on the shoulder before he could say a word. "I guess Eddie does know how to be polite after all."

Liza giggled. "It's just as Great-uncle George said. Eddie is helping a lady in need."

Melody giggled. "Maybe we can find the turkey while Eddie cleans up."

"But we wanted to play soccer with Melody," one of the little cousins said.

"We heard you were a soccer champion," another one said.

"Won't you teach us how to play better?" a third one begged.

Maybe later?

"I can't right now," Melody said. "We have to look for the turkey."

Liza's eyes grew big. "Great-uncle George said Melody would miss a soccer game," she said.

"That doesn't mean anything," Howie said. But Melody didn't look so sure.

"How do you find a turkey?" Melody asked.

Liza shrugged her shoulders. "Let's try pretending we're turkeys and maybe that will help. Follow me."

"Gobble, gobble," Liza said.

"Gobble, gobble," Melody said.

"Gobble, gobble," Howie said.

Eddie didn't gobble. He complained. "Grumble, grumble, grumble," Eddie muttered as he swept crumbs from the floor. "I can't believe I'm stuck here sweeping," he said. "I bet I could find that turkey."

9

TROUBLE WITH A CAPITAL T

"Oh, no!" Liza's mother screamed from the kitchen.

Eddie stopped cleaning. He met Liza, Melody, and Howie in the kitchen. Liza's mother stood near the kitchen table. She pointed underneath it.

Two dogs stared back. Between them was the turkey.

You're in Trouble!

"Who let THEM in here?"
her mother asked.

Liza's face turned white.
Then it turned red.

"They were c...c...cold,"
she stammered.

Liza's mother shook her
finger. "You are in big trouble,
young lady. Trouble with a
capital T!"

Melody gasped. "It's what Great-uncle George said would happen."

Howie nodded. "Maybe Great-uncle George really is a wizard! But remember what he said about me? There's no way that will happen."

Just then, one of the dogs grabbed the turkey and ran toward the door.

Nooooo!

"Noooooo!" Liza's mother screamed.

Eddie pushed Howie aside.
"This is a job for a football star."
Eddie tackled the dog in mid-air.

Well, at least he tried to.
The dog twisted just in time.
Eddie slipped on the floor. His
feet went one way. He went
another. Then Eddie landed
flat on his belly. The turkey
went flying.

"Catch that turkey!" Melody screamed.

And that's exactly what Howie did.

"Everything he said came true," Melody said. The four friends were huddled in Liza's room while the kitchen was being cleaned. "Liza got in trouble. Eddie helped Liza's mother. I turned down a game of soccer. And Howie caught the turkey just like it was a football."

"So what?" Eddie griped. "The turkey was ruined. And so is Thanksgiving."

Just then, the door to Liza's room swung open. There stood Great-uncle George. He still wore his apron and the big chef's hat. He waved his wooden spoon through the air as he spoke. "Dinner is ready," he said. "Hurry, so you won't be late!"

"It'll probably be something terrible like creamed peas and cooked spinach," Eddie griped as they headed down the stairs. But Eddie was wrong. Very wrong.

The dining room table was piled high with a feast. Right in the middle was the biggest turkey ever.

"Where did it all come from?" Melody asked.

Great-uncle George waved his wooden spoon in the air. "Oh, it's just a little something I whipped up!"

Everyone ate until they were full. Soon there was nothing on the table but a pile of dirty dishes.

It was nothing.

"What a mess," Liza said. Melody nodded. "It will take forever to clean this up."

"Don't worry about a thing," Great-uncle George said. "I'll have these done in a snap."

"Do you think Great-uncle George is REALLY a wizard?" Liza asked as the four friends ran outside.

"Only a wizard could create a turkey like that out of nothing," Howie pointed out.

"And it would take a wizard to clean up that mess all by himself," Melody added.

Howie grinned. "This was the best Thanksgiving ever. A great turkey and..."

"A great wizard!" Liza agreed.

Eddie patted his full stomach. "And wizards like your Great-uncle George are welcome in Bailey City any time!"